Put Down Your Phone!

By William Kelly

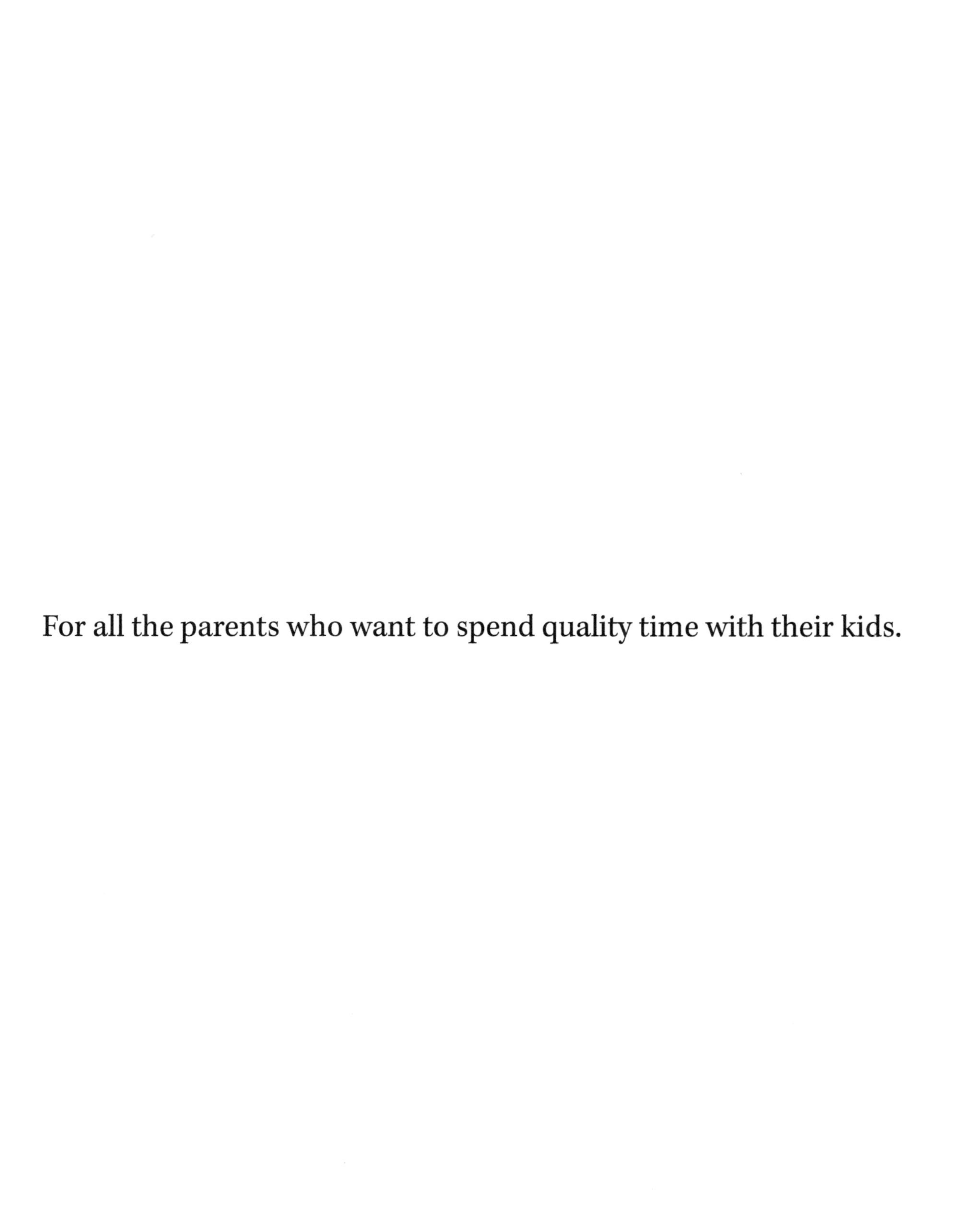

For all the parents who want to spend quality time with their kids.

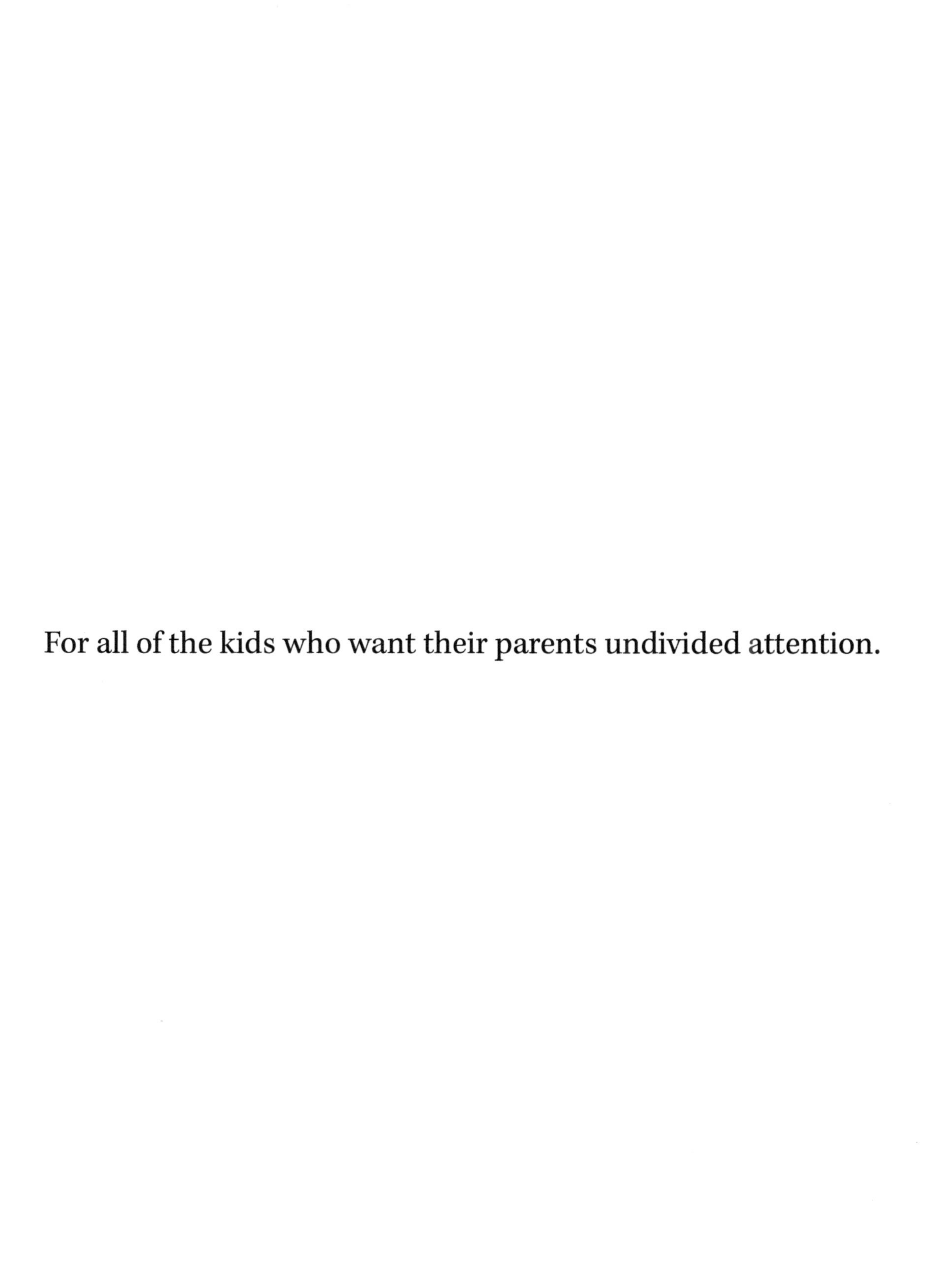

For all of the kids who want their parents undivided attention.

My Dad is always working and has no time for fun.
He is always in his office and never plays in the sun.

He is often very busy and we never get to play.
I feel so sorry for him because he's on his phone all day.

He misses so many of my games, even when he is there.
Sitting in the stands, his phone is where he stares.

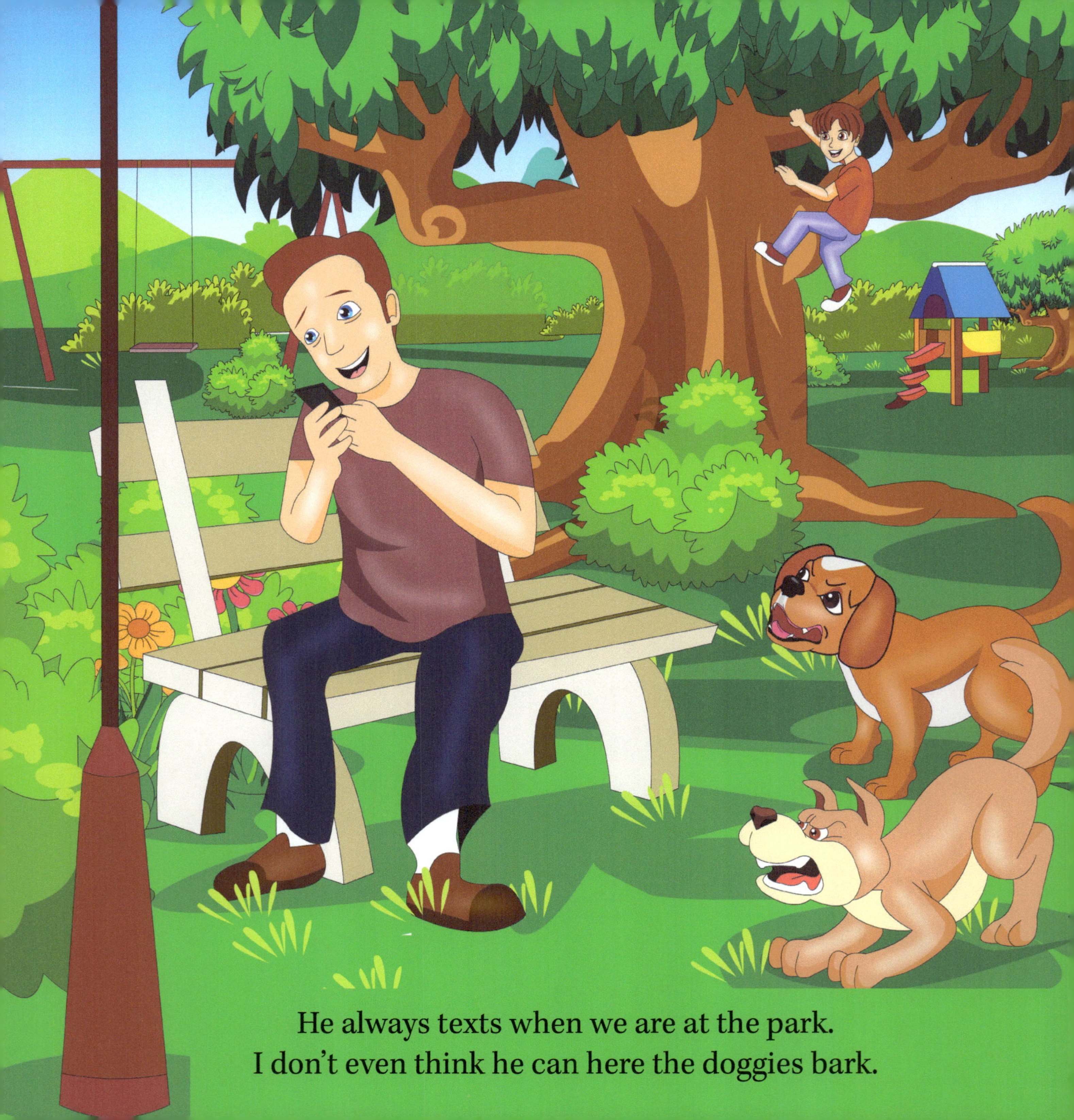

He always texts when we are at the park.
I don't even think he can here the doggies bark.

When it's time for dinner, we don't get much time to talk.
My Dad just keeps on working, his family he forgot.

"So, Doctor can you help him?" I cannot help but worry.
We need to do something about his phone, please help him in a hurry.

I think I know who we can call, it might just do the trick.
We can call a specialist, I think his plan might stick.

Let's call the cell phone doctor, he will know just what to do.
He's helped so many families, I think it will work for you.

The doctor came the next day, in his fancy car.
He cares about his patients, nowhere is too far.

He helps out all the parents, with this serious affliction.
Some people even say it's more like an addiction.

The first thing he always does is assess the situation.
So, the doctor observed my dad in various locations.

He watched him at the movies and even at the mall.
Dad's eyes were glued to his phone, he almost had a fall.

The doctor followed him to school, it was parent's night.
My Dads lack of focus, gave him a little fright.

He examined my Dad at soccer practice and also at the zoo.
The doctor had seen this problem before and knew exactly what to do.

With a scalpel and kind words, he will remove his phone.
This will be done with no loss of blood or bone.

The doctor gave him strict instructions as part of his aftercare.
My Dad must follow them exactly or he will shave off all his hair.

When my Dad gets home from work
this is what he must do.
He must begin by putting down his phone
and then remove his shoes.

Dad broke the rules one day, set by that doctor friend of mine.
He left him with a shiny head, I think he looks just fine

When Dad comes home he leaves the phone, to sit upon the shelf.
So that he can spend time with his kids and improve his health.

These days I have my Dad's complete attention.
He loves to hear about my day, even if I got detention.

My Dad seems so much happier now and truthfully so am I.
That doctor did some amazing work he is one amazing guy.

For all you Moms and Dads out there who are always on your phone.
Turn it off, put them away as soon as you get home.

It's time for you to teach your kids how to listen and to talk.
Make memories together, go for ice cream or a walk.

Ask yourself what's more important, your kids of your phone?
Before you even know it, they will be moving away from home.

So, think about what you have taught them
and the way that you behave.
Is your phone more important,
or is it fond memories that you crave?

Thank you

About the Author

William Kelly is a father, author and international educator with over a decade of experience working in the health and fitness industry. He has an honors degree in kinesiology/ physical education and a master's degree in international education administration. William has helped to develop a variety of Health and Physical Education curriculums for international schools around the world. His passion is helping children find enjoyment and confidence in being physically active. He consistently works with children and their families to live healthy active lifestyles.

9 781796 632361